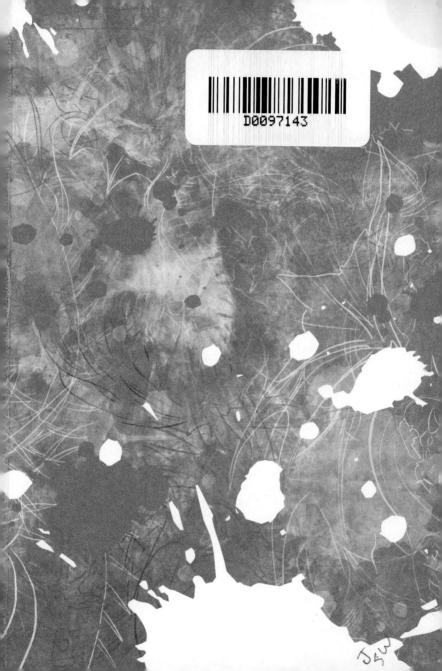

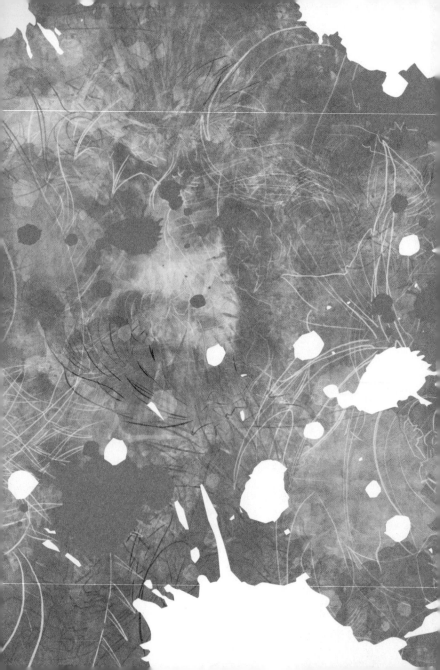

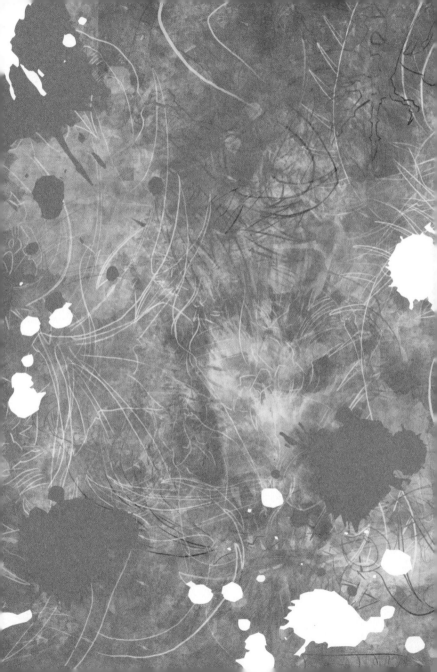

DRAGONBLOOD
IT SCREAMS AT NIGHT

Michael Dahl

Yap Kun Rong

STONE ARCH BOOKS
www.stonearchbooks.com

Zone Books are published by
Stone Arch Books
A Capstone Imprint
151 Good Counsel Drive, P.O. Box 669
Mankato, Minnesota 56002
www.capstonepub.com

Library of Congress Cataloging-in-Publication Data
Dahl, Michael.
    It Screams at Night / by Michael Dahl; illustrated by
Yap Kun Rong.
    p. cm. — (Zone Books. Dragonblood)
    ISBN 978-1-4342-1261-0 (library binding)
    ISBN 978-1-4342-2311-1 (softcover)
    [1. Dragons—Fiction.] I. Kun Rong, Yap, ill. II. Title.
PZ7.D15134It 2009
[Fic]—dc22
                                            2008031282

Summary: A lonely farmhouse on a deserted dirt road
holds a terrible secret. A young boy is held captive by
his family. But it's for his own good. They are trying to
protect him from a dangerous creature. A creature that
screams in the night.

Creative Director: Heather Kindseth
Graphic Designer: Brann Garvey

Printed in the United States of America in Stevens Point, Wisconsin.
012011
006068R

TABLE OF CONTENTS

Introduction

A new Age of Dragons is about to begin. The powerful creatures will return to rule the world once more, but this time will be different. This time, they will have allies. Who will help them? Around the world, some young humans are making a strange discovery. They are learning that they were born with dragon blood — blood that gives them amazing powers.

CHAPTER 1
Strange Blood

A van stopped near a lonely farmhouse in northern Canada.

The van was a **bloodmobile**.

During the day, the driver drove to schools and hospitals so that people could donate blood.

This afternoon, the driver turned off the van and checked her records.

A teenage boy named Sam Stevens had donated blood at a high school last week.

But there was something strange about the donation.

Sam Stevens had lizard **blood** in
his veins.

"There must be a mistake," the
driver said to herself.

The driver wanted to talk to
Sam Stevens.

She believed the boy needed to
see a doctor.

The driver walked up to the front door.

The *windows* of the house were **dark.**

When she knocked, there was
no answer.

Then she saw a *light* moving
through the forest.

CHAPTER 2
THE TOWER

Someone was walking among
the trees next to the farmhouse.

Quietly, the driver walked into
the woods.

As she got closer to the *light*,
the driver saw a man.

The man was carrying food
on a tray.

He also held a lantern and
a rifle.

The man walked through the
trees toward a stone tower.

The driver followed him.

A clanking sound came from
inside the tower.

CHAPTER 3
IN CHAINS

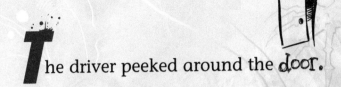

The driver peeked around the door.

The man placed the tray of food on the floor.

A teenage boy sat in front of the man.

The boy was **chained** to the wall of the tower.

"Who came up the driveway?" asked the boy.

"Never mind," said the man. "Eat your dinner, Sam."

Suddenly, Sam began to **shake**. The chains **rattled**.

"I can't stay here forever," he cried.

"It's for your own protection,"

said the man.

Sam looked down at the strange **birthmark** on his arm.

"I'm different," he said. "I can't change that. It's in my **blood**."

Then Sam added *quietly*, "They're coming for me. I know they are."

CHAPTER 4

DRAGON CRY

Something **roared** in the forest.

Sam began to sweat.

As the driver watched, wings sprouted from the boy's back.

Sharp claws grew out of his fingers.

Sam's face became long and pointed.

Another roar **shook** the forest.

"I'll never let them take you away," said the man.

He grabbed his rifle.

The driver, standing at the door, turned around.

Behind her stood a scaly creature with wings.

It was a dragon.

The driver ran inside the tower as the dragon lunged forward.

Its huge jaws pushed against the doorway.

The man used his rifle to attack the creature.

The dragon was not scared off.

The small dragon that used to be Sam pulled against the chains.

Both creatures roared at each other.

All night the **large dragon** tried to enter the tower.

The driver and the man worked together to fight the creature.

Then a mighty wind shook the forest.

Trees groaned and creaked.

The huge dragon turned and flew off into the night sky.

Sam returned to his normal shape.

He lay, tired and sweating, on the floor of the tower.

"I told you I wouldn't let them get you, Sam," said the man.

Sam *smiled* weakly.

"It'll be back," said Sam.

"And I'll be waiting for it," said

the man.

He turned to the driver and said,

"Lucky for us you were here."

When Sam fell asleep, the
driver stepped outside.

Morning *light* began to fill the
peaceful forest.

Will it be peaceful tomorrow night?
she wondered.

Of Dragons and Near-Dragons

If dragons lived on Earth, they would probably communicate with each other the way other reptiles do.

Many reptiles hiss by blowing air through their mouths.

Snakes can hear a human speaking from 10 feet away. Some scientists believe that snakes can also feel vibrations from other snakes miles away.

The **tuatara** (too-uh-TAR-uh) lizard of New Zealand has no outside ears. But it can still hear!

Some lizards communicate by doing push-ups! They bob up and down to warn other lizards to stay away from their territory.

Baby alligators chirp inside their eggs. They tell their mothers it is time to dig up the eggs from the dirt. They are ready to hatch!

ABOUT THE AUTHOR

Michael Dahl is the author of more than 200 books for children and young adults. He has won the AEP Distinguished Achievement Award three times for his nonfiction. His Finnegan Zwake mystery series was shortlisted twice by the Anthony and Agatha awards. He has also written the *Library of Doom* series. He is a featured speaker at conferences around the country on graphic novels and high-interest books for boys.

ABOUT THE ILLUSTRATOR

Yap Kun Rong is a freelance illustrator and concept artist for books, comics, and video games. He lives and works in Tokyo, Japan.

GLOSSARY

allies (AL-eyez)—people or countries that give support to each other

birthmark (BURTH-mark)—a mark on the skin that was there from birth

creaked (KREEKD)—made a squeaky, grating noise

creature (KREE-chur)—a living thing that is human or animal

donate (DOH-nate)—give something freely. A donation is a gift that is given without getting a reward.

lunged (LUHNJD)—moved forward quickly and suddenly

rule (ROOL)—have power over something

sprouted (SPROUT-id)—grew, appeared, or developed quickly

DISCUSSION QUESTIONS

1. Do you think it was smart for the driver to go to the farmhouse? Why or why not?

2. What or who did you think was locked in the tower? Explain your answer.

3. If you were the author, what would you have named this book? Why?

WRITING PROMPTS

1. The author gives a couple of clues that Sam is a dragon. Find the clues and make a list.

2. Why do you think the other dragon was trying to get Sam? Write a paragraph explaining your reasons.

3. What do you think would have happened to Sam and the man if the driver hadn't been there? Rewrite the ending without the driver.

INTERNET SITES

The book may be over, but the adventure
is just beginning.

Do you want to read more about the
subjects or ideas in this book? Want to
play cool games or watch videos about
the authors who write these books? Then
go to FactHound. At *www.facthound.com*,
you'll be able to do all that, and more.
The FactHound website can also send you
to other safe Internet sites.

Check it out!

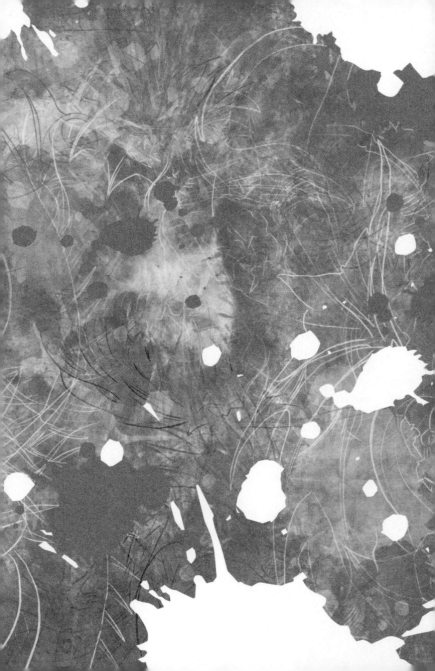

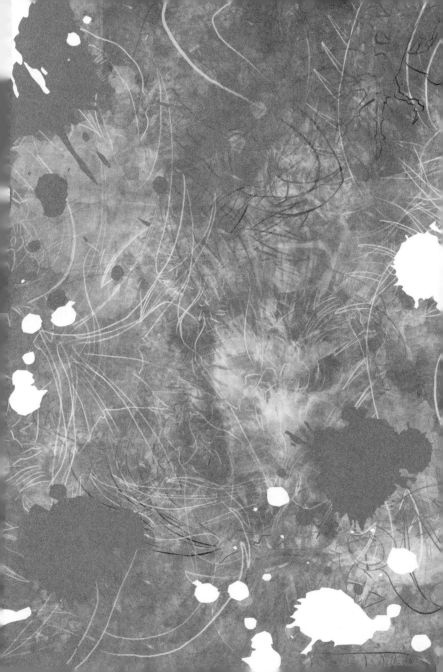